For Emily Francesca

Text copyright © 1996 Geoffrey Trease
Illustrations copyright © 1996 Pauline Hazelwood

The right of Geoffrey Trease to be identified as the author
of this Work and the right of Pauline Hazelwood to be
identified as the illustrator of this Work has been asserted
to them in accordance with the Copyright, Designs and
Patents Act 1988.

This edition first published in Great Britain in 1996
by Macdonald Young Books Ltd

Typeset in 16/24 Meridien by Roger Kohn Designs
Printed and bound in Belgium by Proost N. V.

Macdonald Young Books Ltd.
61 Western Road
Hove
East Sussex BN3 1JD

British Library Cataloguing in Publications Data available

ISBN 0 7500 2112 8
ISBN 0 7500 2113 6   (pb)

Geoffrey Trease

Page to
Jane Seymour

Illustrated by Pauline Hazelwood

MACDONALD YOUNG BOOKS

1
Never 'No' to a King

"Not a man – a monster," my mother cried.

Father was horrified. "That word could ruin us all. Shut the door, Francis – make sure there's no one outside."

I rushed across the parlour. Our servants do not listen behind doors. I went back to my parents.

"I am not shouting anything from the housetops," said my mother more quietly. "Just reminding you of the facts."

"Very well, my dear. But..." Father hesitated, glancing at me.

"Let the boy stay. It concerns him more than anyone."

"Very well. But you won't repeat what we say, lad?"

"No, sir." By now I was bursting with curiosity.

"The simple facts," said Mother. "The Queen – the late queen we must say now, God rest her soul. Anne Boleyn. Died just ten days ago. Died? Put to death! Her head cut off in the Tower. By order of her gracious husband, King Henry the Eighth."

"Careful," Father warned her.

It was not news to me. For the past week the servants had talked of little else. She had been unfaithful to the King. It was hard to believe that the stories were all true. Yet four men had been tried, tortured, and put to death, before the Queen herself had been made to kneel blindfolded before the executioner.

"The very next day," Mother went on, "the King announced that he was to take a new wife, her lady-in-waiting, Jane Seymour. And tomorrow – only eleven days later! – they will be married in the Palace of Whitehall."

I remembered something Father had said. "This concerns me?" I asked puzzled.

He picked up an open letter with the royal seal. "There is to be a clean sweep in the household," my mother explained. "Jane Seymour was a lady-in-waiting to Queen Anne. She can't possibly be attended by those she used to work with."

As I still looked baffled Father made a joke of it. "Even the King can't turn **you** into a lady-in-waiting. But he wants you to become one of the queen's pages."

Mother said grimly: "He wishes to honour your father. You know what friends they were as boys."

I had heard many stories of those days. Father had been one of the little hand-picked group Henry the Seventh had thought suitable to share his son's lessons.

Father had stayed at court until they were both eighteen. Then Henry the Seventh had died, the prince had been crowned Henry the Eighth, and had instantly married Katherine of Aragon. The King had remembered their friendship and meant this as a favour.

I was utterly amazed. "What do you think, Mother?" I could guess. "It's not for me to think," she said.

"This letter must be answered at once," said Father. "You do not keep a king waiting. And you never say no to one."

2
A Boat Down River

Two days later Father hired a Thames waterman to take us down to Greenwich. Seeing the Tower ramparts as we passed London Bridge I shuddered to remember Queen Anne's death a few weeks before.

Father had made it clearer why great persons were not always as free as others to do as they liked. They must think of what was best for their country.

It was vital for a king to have a son to follow him. Never yet in history had England accepted a daughter. Without a son it had meant civil war between other male relatives. When Henry's father had won his crown in battle, at Bosworth, it had cost thousands of lives.

Young Henry's first wife, Katherine of Aragon, had brought him only Mary, and no prospect of more babies.

Henry wanted to get out of the marriage. But the Church did not allow divorce. When he asked the Pope to annul the marriage – say it did not count, it had never been legal – the Pope refused and they had a terrible quarrel. In the end Henry had gone his own way, defied the Pope, and married Anne Boleyn.

She had a baby. But only another girl, Elizabeth. "Only", because a daughter did not solve Henry's worrying problem.

The stubborn English would not want a woman to rule them. Henry had a nightmare vision of battles and bloodshed.

He had another reason for wanting to end this second marriage. Anne was young and flighty. People said she had love-affairs with younger men whom she preferred to Henry, who was old enough to be her own father.

Suppose Anne did have a boy, now – who could be sure that it was the King's child? It was high treason for a queen to be unfaithful.

That gossip, true or false, lay behind Anne's execution. I saw why Mother had been horrified and disgusted with the King. But Father had shown me that Henry was not just a mindless monster. He had reasons driving him to what he had just done.

Now Greenwich Palace crept into view along the curve of the south bank. It brought back to Father a rush of boyhood memories spent here with the prince.

Another of that group who shared their lessons had been Dudley Collett, one of the high officers who met us when we stepped ashore. Sir Dudley had clung to that early link with Henry. He had been climbing steadily ever since. My father had not that sort of ambition.

I asked Sir Dudley just what a page's duties were. "Shall I be up to them?"

He laughed. "What do you do? You do as you are told. Instantly! You'll see when to kneel. When in doubt, bow. Go out of the Queen's presence backwards – and the King's, of course. And don't fall. Simple!" He roared with laughter.

3
Leopards and Panthers

Henry changed everything in his bride's apartments.

In every window Anne Boleyn's emblem, the leopard, must be replaced by Jane Seymour's badge, a panther. The royal engraver rushed breathless from room to room.

But the new queen was no panther. I took to her at once. So kind, so young and attractive, almost motherly to her royal stepdaughters neither of whom now had a real mother of her own.

23

Princess Mary was grown up, nineteen. Her mother, the Catholic Katherine of Aragon, had died months earlier.

But Elizabeth, a grey-eyed, reddish-gold little girl, still under three, had lost **her** mother, the Protestant Anne Boleyn, only a few weeks ago – in a terrible scene, beheaded as a traitor on Tower Green.

I was relieved to realise that queens seldom saw as much of their own children as most parents did. Court life was too full. I scarcely heard Elizabeth mention Anne.

The Countess of Salisbury had come to reorganize the household for Jane. She was a rather grand person, herself of royal blood, so she could keep us all in order. Under her were all the ladies of the bedchamber, the younger ones known as maids of honour.

They waited on the queen's most ordinary needs. One held her washbasin, another her towel. Others braided or brushed her hair, helped her to dress and undress. It was an honour to do the simplest service. Nothing was left to common servants.

Such duties of course were not for us pages. But for most of the waking hours the queen's splendid bedchamber became almost a public place, with people constantly in and out. So, if we were to serve her, we too must be in and out, making ourselves useful or amusing. There were games, there was singing and music and reading of books.

I at once made friends with the youngest maid of honour. Ursula was just my age.

After the recent tragic happenings we knew it was vital to make this a happy home now. Jane was a bride. She really was in love with the King. We must do our small best to help.

And when Henry himself came
striding in, laughing and slapping his
hands and flinging his huge arms round
her, it was sheer magic.

I saw now my father's friend of long
ago. Why he had so much admired
this hearty high-spirited prince – the
ringleader in every sport and game, the
best rider and dancer, the life and soul
of every party.

Henry had always been enormous for his age, but they had not thought of him as fat. He had always enjoyed his food and drink. Now he had thickened out with age.

He adored his new queen. If only things would go more happily for him now! Ursula and I saw every hope for the new family they would make together.

He was always warm with the two girls. But now, with luck, Jane would bear the son he so much longed for.

4
The Pilgrimage of Grace

A golden summer that was!
The court moved round from
one palace to another of the half-dozen
encircling London – from Greenwich to
Eltham and up-river to Hampton Court,
enjoying the deerparks and special
beauties of each. The famous foreign
artist, Holbein, painted all the royal
family.

"It's sweet to see them," said Ursula.
And it was – Jane slim and graceful,
Henry more than ever like a broad-
shouldered amiable ox, all laughter.
Only oxen do not dress as he did with
his sweeping robes, his flashing jewels
and glittering chains.

Jane had a mind of her own. Which can be awkward if your husband is a king – and one like Henry.

That autumn he had trouble in the North. He was trying to reform some of the old monasteries where monks had grown slack and were neglecting the good works with which they used to help the poor. Like running schools and hospitals.

The King wanted to close down a lot of them. There were riots and uproar, and a great protest march on York, the Pilgrimage of Grace, to save places that had done so much good.

This made Henry furious. What could ignorant common people know about such things, and how his kingdom should be governed?

Jane saw their point of view. She was not against monks and nuns and the old religious ideas as Anne Boleyn had been.

She went down on her knees to plead with him. He burst into a fury – for once angry even with her.

"Get up!" he stormed. His eyes grew small and piggy. "Don't meddle with matters that don't concern you."

She had to obey. But Ursula and I felt sure she would find some way to soften him.

5
Christmas Was Coming

The news got better. Or perhaps there was just less dismal news from the North, where the bad weather and vile road conditions meant that few messengers got south to us.

We in London heard little of those savage outbreaks so far away or the bitter punishments and even executions with which the King's officers were told to put them down. Our talk was all of the good time we should have at Christmas.

The King always liked to spend this
time at Greenwich. The court would go
down in a splendid long procession of
boats from Westminster, but this year
the weather even in London made that
impossible. The river was frozen at
London Bridge. The ice spread from bank
to bank, thick enough to bear the weight
of huts and stalls and sideshows of every
kind. The Thames could have a frost fair
as it sometimes did.

There would be dancing and sliding and sledging, music everywhere, torchlight after dark, casks of ale and wine, even meat roasting above sheets of metal that protected the ice below.

But no chance of a procession of boats!

"Never mind," cried Henry jovially. "We shall ride down from Westminster and cross by the Bridge."

So we all rode in splendour, the full length of the City, calling at St. Paul's for a service of thanksgiving. The Queen rode on one side and Princess Mary, proud and dignified on the other. As we went over the arched bridge afterwards we got glimpses of the fair spread below us.

At Greenwich it was all one festivity from New Year's Eve to Twelfth Night.

Then very soon we in the Queen's household got the first whisper of the news: Queen Jane was to have a baby.

We all felt certain that the King would get his wish this time – a son. A prince to follow him, and remove the risk that England would face the problem of a female ruler.

London went wild with joy at the thought. Bonfires blazed on every street corner. By each stood barrels of wine, with people lining up at each to fill their mugs as long as a drop remained.

Henry always wanted everyone to have a good time.

6
Bonfires and Bells

What a long wait we had till October! But we never doubted that this time our strong-willed King would have his desire granted.

Jane was to have her baby at Hampton Court, and superb apartments were got ready. The child seemed in no hurry to be born. Some of the ladies got worried. In the City there was a solemn procession round the churches to pray that all would be well.

At two o'clock in the morning, on 12 October, I must have been one of the first to get the news.

I read it in Ursula's radiant eyes when she came out of the bedchamber into the anteroom where I was dozing at my duty.

We had to be so careful, ourselves, not to speak a word, we young ones. But the girl's face told me everything. All was well! It was a boy.

None of the King's preparations would be wasted. The tournament planned in the baby's honour would be held in all its glittering splendour, with knights in armour and bearing bright lances like wands.

London gave itself up to rejoicings. The bonfires blazed, the wine ran like fountains. Bells rang from every church tower and steeple across the wide city.

Guns boomed from the batteries of the Tower, thunderous – two thousand shots were fired.

Little Edward – Edward the Sixth as we knew him in later years – was christened with Princess Mary as godmother and his little half-sister as witness. And when the King took the baby in his arms he was weeping openly with joy.

Three days later Edward was proclaimed Prince of Wales. But a week later, at midnight, poor Jane died and left him motherless. Her dream was over.

The royal household broke up again. Ursula and I were packed off to our homes.

"I hope we meet again," I said sadly.

"I have a feeling we shall," she said.